T0380511

GRANDMA'S
MAGIC BLANKET

Written by

Mary Cecilia Freeman

Illustrated by

Tanya Maneki

To order additional copies of this book, contact:
Xlibris
1-888-795-4274
www.Xlibris.com
Orders@Xlibris.com

ISBN: Softcover   978-1-7960-8158-9
       Hardcover   978-1-7960-8159-6
       EBook   978-1-7960-8157-2

Print information available on the last page

Rev. date: 01/08/2020

DEDICATED TO
MY MOM

What better gift to give
to your loved ones then
a large cozy blanket.

Blankets are like the arms
that hug you and keep you
safe and sound at night.

Soft and gentle, full of
color and shapes. Blankets
are magical. Especially the
ones Grandma makes.

GRANDMA
DOESN'T KNOW ME
YET BUT SHE'S
SUPER EXCITED
TO MEET ME.

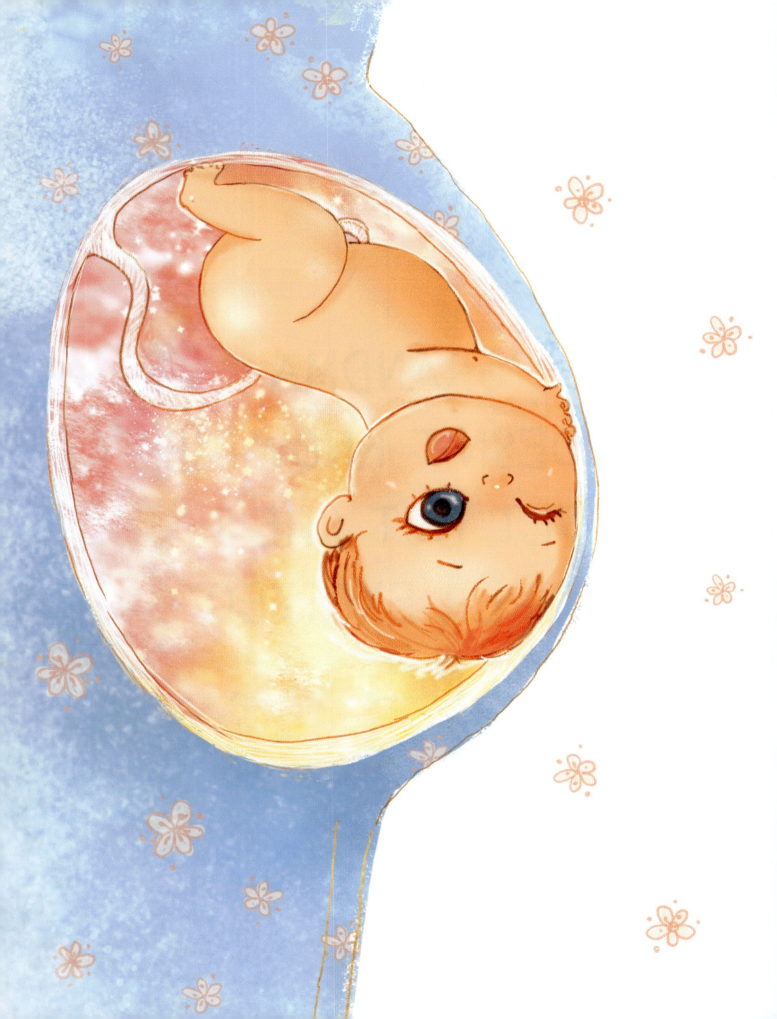

I HEAR HER VOICE ALL THE TIME. SHE'S MAKING ME SOMETHING CALLED A BLANKET.

IT SOUNDS BIG
AND MAGICAL. SHE
SAID THERE'S
GOING TO BE A LOT
OF IT.

SHE SAYS I'M GOING TO LOVE IT BECAUSE IT'S GOING TO BE PINK AND WARM. PERFECT FOR NEWBORNS SHE SAYS.

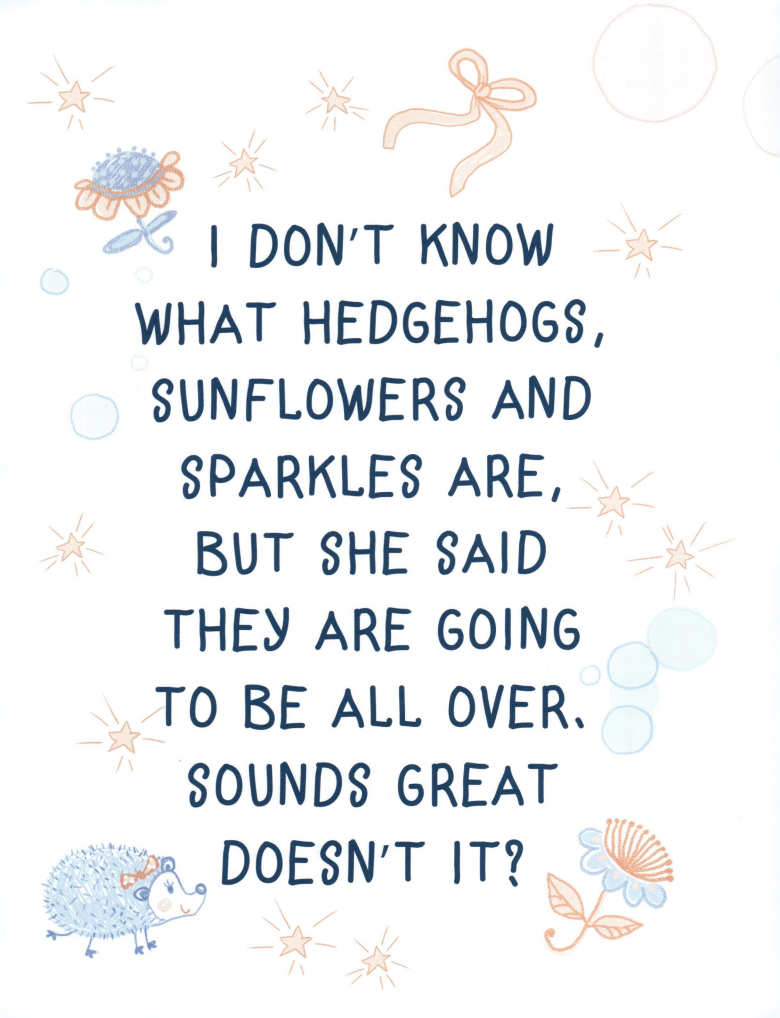

I DON'T KNOW WHAT HEDGEHOGS, SUNFLOWERS AND SPARKLES ARE, BUT SHE SAID THEY ARE GOING TO BE ALL OVER. SOUNDS GREAT DOESN'T IT?

MOMMY SAYS IT'S PERFECT AND SHE CAN'T WAIT TO WRAP ME UP IN IT. I WONDER WHAT THIS BLANKET WILL LOOK LIKE.

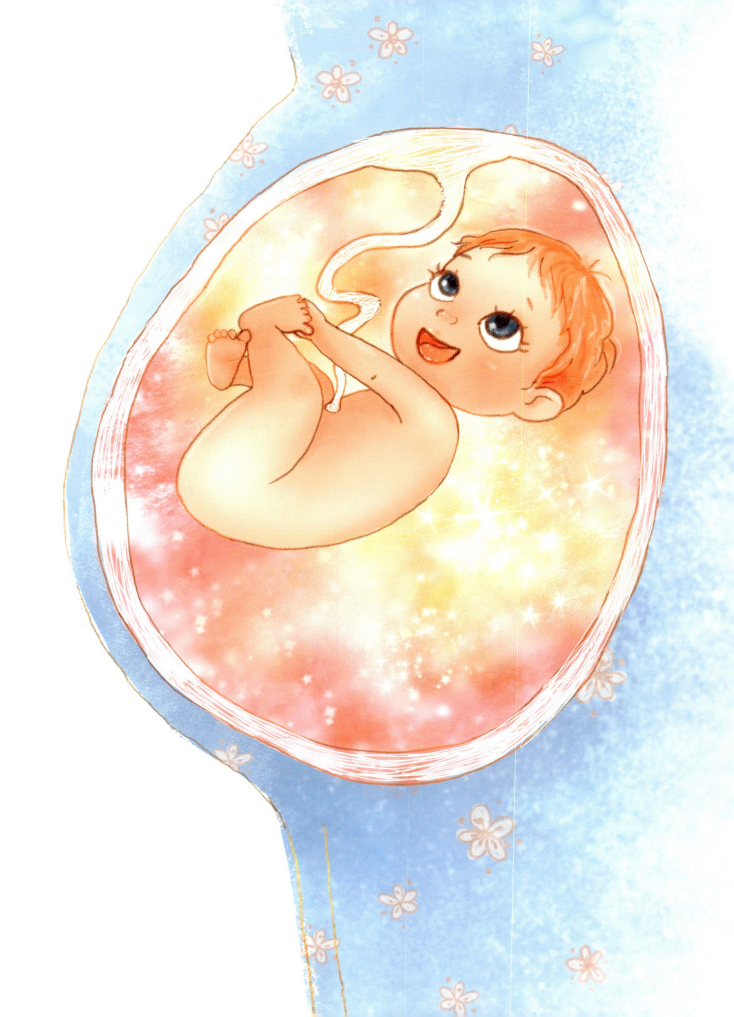

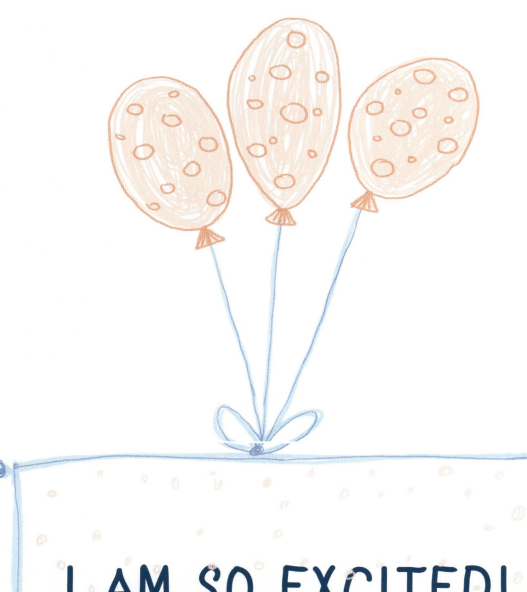

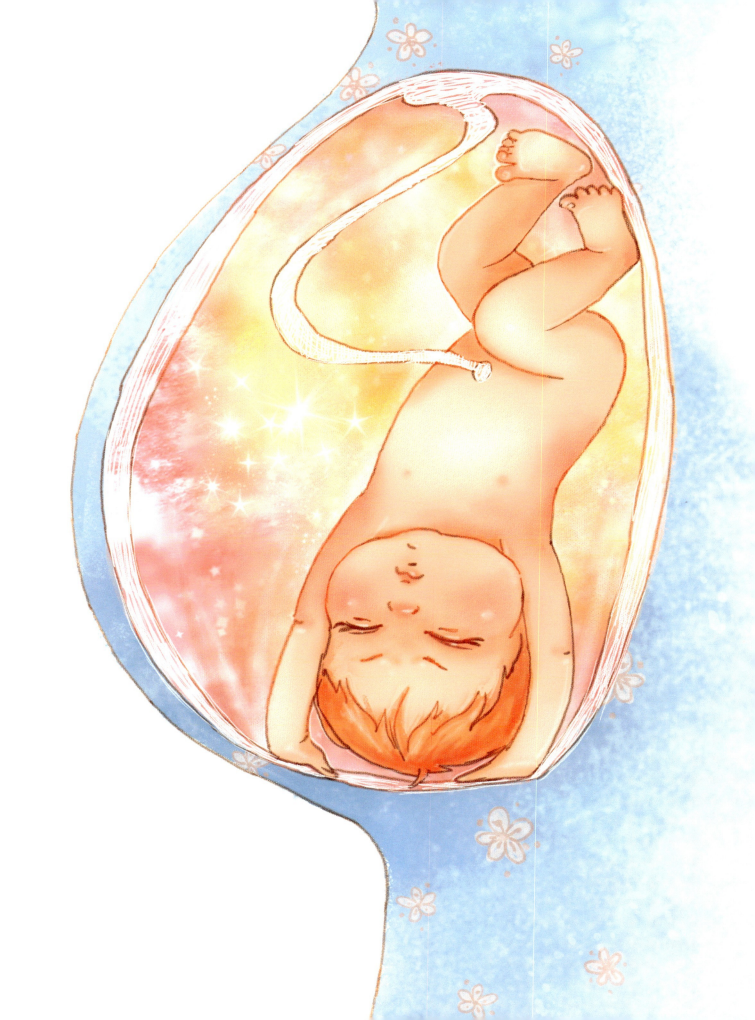

AFTER MEETING MOMMY AND DADDY, I GOT TO MEET GRANDMA AND GRANDPA.

MOMMY AND GRANDMA ARE RIGHT, I LOVE MY MAGICAL BLANKET!

THE
END

Printed in the United States
By Bookmasters